# Do Tigers

### illustrated by MARIO RIVOLI

# Ever Bite Kings?

text by BARBARA WERSBA

Atheneum   New York   1968

The Queen was bored . . .

For the King was asleep,
Dreaming dreams that were blissfully deep.
The taxes were paid and the halls were swept
But the Queen was angry because the King slept.

She tugged at his beard and pinched him three times
To silence the sound of his snoring.
"Wake up!" she declared. "And amuse me at once,
For I find you incredibly boring."

The King woke at once and did a small dance,
Thinking a polka would please her.
He twirled on his toes and gave her a rose
But nothing like this would appease her.

"Shall we play checkers?" he patiently asked.
"You are dull, you are stupid," she said.
"I'm bored, I'm bored, I'm so thoroughly bored
I'm ready to stand on my head."

The Baker, the Poet, the Prince, and the Fool
Heard at once of this terrible plight.
And drawing together they started to plan
To make the dilemma come right.

"Our glorious Queen mustn't stand on her head!"
  The Poet began to declaim.
"It's a highly undignified posture
  That is certain to damage the brain."

"Then give her a unicorn tied to a leash,"
  Said the Prince, "or a friendly giraffe."
"Or take her away in a great big balloon,"
  Said the Poet. "It might make her laugh."

"Fa la la," said the Baker, beginning to waltz,
"Let me go to my oven and bake.
  The only sure cure for an upside-down Queen
  Is a pineapple upside-down cake."

"Fools!" said the Fool. "You're misguided.
  Our Queen has no use for balloons.
  And a friendly giraffe would merely be dull
  Unless it could sing a few tunes.

"As for unicorns, they are outmoded,
  And a pineapple cake is too sweet.
  What *I* recommend is a TIGER HUNT:
  A diversion that could be complete."

"A Tiger Hunt!" said the Poet with joy,
"Why didn't we see that before?"
"A TIGER, A TIGER," the Baker exclaimed.
"She couldn't say that was a bore!"

(The four agreed and with lightning speed
  Knocked on the King's chamber door.)

The Queen was completely delighted
And started to pack up her things.
But the King felt dreadfully worried.
Did Tigers ever bite Kings?

Now here was a question of import,
  And the King mulled it round in his head.
"If they *don't* bite, I'm safe," he decided.
"If they *do* bite, I'm certainly dead."

After reading some guidebooks on jungles,
Their Majesties promptly got dressed.
The Queen wore her very best hunting hat
And the King wore a tiger-striped vest.

A golden coach was made ready
And the King, just on a hunch,
Packed in with the guns and helmets and nets,
Some blueberry muffins for lunch.

"Be brave," said the Poet. "Be bold," said the Fool.
"Be *fierce*," said the Prince to the King.
"I'll try," said the King, all a-tremble,
"But I really can't promise a thing."

The King and the Queen and their party
Galloped off to their hunting domains.
"The sky's very gray," said the King in dismay,
"Do Tigers bite more when it rains?"

They came to an olive-green jungle
Where cockatoos shrieked in the trees.
The King thought the noise came from Tigers
And started to quake in the knees.

"Good grief," said the Queen, "you look frightful.
Blow your nose, fix your socks, load your gun.
Stop trembling, stop shaking, stop quaking.
We are here, my good man, to have fun!"

The King and the Queen, with some effort,
Climbed onto the branch of a tree.
But though they kept watch for a Tiger,
Not a single one did they see.

"I'm hungry," the King moaned. "I'm tired.
It's time for my afternoon nap."
"Hush!" said the Queen. "Watch for Tigers,
Or I'll give you a very hard rap."

"Watch for Tigers," the King echoed weakly.
  But this he was thinking instead:
"If they *don't* bite, I've no need to worry,
  If they *do* bite, I'll quickly be dead."

  Quite suddenly, out of the bushes,
  A head appeared, and a tail.
"A TIGER," shouted the others,
  But the King could only turn pale.

"My goodness," he said. "Is it really?
    O gentlemen, surely you're wrong.
    That can't be a genuine Tiger,
    For the tip of his tail is too long.

"His ears are too big, his nose is too black,
    He has a strange look in the eyes.
    His stripes don't seem to be where they should,
    I think it's a zebra disguised!"

    But the Queen had fired her rifle,
    And the Tiger leaped in alarm.
"Chase him, good King," cried the others,
    "He'll do you no permanent harm."

Before he could hide in the branches,
Before he could climb to the top,
The King gave a shriek and fell from the tree.
He hit with a terrible plop.

"That way, over there," they all shouted.
And the King, with a pain in his head,
Began to run after the Tiger,
Longing for hot milk and bed.

He ran desperately into the bushes,
And aimed at one black beady eye,
When the Tiger, deeply alarmed and upset,
Stopped short and started to cry.

"Now, now!" said the King. "What's the matter?"
And forgetting all of his fears,
He walked right up to the Tiger
And brushed away one of his tears.

"I'm tired," the Tiger said sadly,
"Of pretending to be very bold.
For I have a delicate stomach
And I *may* be getting a cold."

"Poor beast," said the King. "Poor old Tiger.
　Why, I feel the same way as you!
　I *hate* hunting Tigers in jungles,
　But my wife is a bit of a shrew.

"You see, I'm a miserable coward.
　I was even afraid you might bite.
　But now that I've met you, I truly believe
　That Tigers and Kings are alike."

"So they are!" said the Tiger with pleasure.
"And now sir, just fire your gun.
　I'll utter the cry of a Tiger forlorn
　And they'll certainly think you have won."

"How generous," the King said. "How thoughtful."
　And he blasted his gun at the sky.
"Help help!" screamed the Tiger. "I'm wounded!
　I think I'm beginning to die."

　The King drew a sword from the sash at his waist,
　And the Tiger kneeled on the grass.
"I dub you," the King said, "by law of the land,
　An Excellent Tiger, First Class.

"A Tiger of sweetness and courage,
A Tiger of Sensible Heart.
The friend of a King, your praises I'll sing
Till death, noble Tiger, us part."

The King returned to his party
And he kissed the hand of the Queen.
Said he: "My dear, did you happen to hear
Some shots and a rather loud scream?"

"What of it?" she cried. "Where's the Tiger?
Why should I believe what I hear?
Unless I can see for myself that he's dead,
I'll give you a box on the ear.

"I'll tickle your sides, I'll jump on your toes,
I'll take away all of your games.
I'll tell everyone you're a coward
And I'll make you go out when it rains."

The Queen marched away through the bushes,
And the King, badly shaken with fear,
Ran ahead, calling: "Tiger, we're coming.
O Tiger, friend Tiger, we're here."

The Tiger, thank goodness, had heard him
And was lying quite stiff on the ground.
All of his paws were up in the air,
And his silence was deep and profound.

"He is dead!" said the Queen. "So he is," said the rest.
"He is totally, thoroughly dead.
  His tail is quite dead, and also his nose,
  And even the hairs on his head."

"HURRAH," they all shouted. "And bravo.
  Our King is the strongest by far!"
"It's nothing," the King said superbly,
"But let's leave the remains where they are."

The King and the Queen and their party
Rolled back through the streets of the town.
And thousands cheered and threw roses
At the King, who was doffing his crown.

A blast of trumpets was sounded,
And aloft, in letters of gold,
Flew a giant balloon with this message:
OUR KING IS INCREDIBLY BOLD.

At the castle, ten generals were waiting
With champagne and truffles and ice.
"You shouldn't have gone to the bother,"
Smiled the King. "Chocolate cake will suffice."

So the King is at peace, and he naps all he wants.
And the Queen, for the moment, is quiet.
The Baker has baked forty Devil's Food Cakes
Which make up the King's daily diet.

The Poet has called him the bravest of men
And has written some very brave poems.
The Fool has composed a long essay
Called "Tigers, Their Habits And Homes."

The castle's been painted a bright jungle-green,
And the Prince, after many requests,
Has ordered the army and all the King's men
To parade wearing tiger-striped vests.

And now, every year in September
The King steals away with great glee
Till he comes to an olive-green jungle
Where he and the Tiger have tea.

They are peaceful there, these old comrades,
For they speak about beautiful things:
Of Kings who befriend gentle Tigers,
And of Tigers who never bite Kings.